El primer invierno de Chaucer

Chaucer's First Winter

For Peter, who has always liked winter.
—S. K.

Para Peter, a quien siempre le ha gustado el invierno.
—S. K.

ACKNOWLEDGMENTS

With many thanks to Laurent and Navah,
for all your help and good humor.
—H. C.

RECONOCIMIENTOS

Con gran agradecimiento para Laurent y Navah,
por toda su ayuda y buen humor.
—H. C.

SIMON & SCHUSTER BOOKS FOR YOUNG READERS
An imprint of Simon & Schuster Children's Publishing Division
1230 Avenue of the Americas, New York, New York 10020
Text copyright © 2008 by Stephen Krensky
Illustrations copyright © 2008 by Henry Cole
The illustrated depiction of the Ty Inc. plush toy bear is used with the permission of Ty Inc. © 2008, Ty Inc.
All rights reserved. TY, the Ty Heart Logo, and TY CLASSIC are all trademarks owned by Ty Inc.
All rights reserved, including the right of reproduction in whole or in part in any form.
Cheerios® and Spoonfuls of Stories® are registered trademarks of General Mills.
SIMON & SCHUSTER BOOKS FOR YOUNG READERS is a trademark of Simon & Schuster, Inc.
For information about special discounts for bulk purchases, please contact Simon & Schuster Special Sales
at 1-866-506-1949 or business@simonandschuster.com.
The Simon & Schuster Speakers Bureau can bring authors to your live event. For more information or to book an event
contact the Simon & Schuster Speakers Bureau at 1-866-248-3049 or visit our website at www.simonspeakers.com.
Book design by Laurent Linn
The text for this book is set in Alghera.
The illustrations for this book are rendered in acrylic paint, colored pencil, and ink on arches hot press water color paper
Manufactured in the United States of America
0610 RRO
2 4 6 8 10 9 7 5 3 1
Library of Congress Cataloging-in-Publication Data
Krensky, Stephen.
Chaucer's first winter / Stephen Krensky ; illustrated by Henry Cole.
— 1st ed.
p.   cm.
Summary: A curious young bear, who does not want to miss the delights of winter,
skips his first hibernation to play in the snow, glide on the ice,
and admire the glittering rows of icicles and snow-covered pine trees.
ISBN 978-1-4169-7479-6 (hardcover)
[1. Bears—Fiction. 2. Hibernation—Fiction. 3. Winter—Fiction.]
I. Cole, Henry, ill. II. Title.
PZ7.K883Cf 2008   [É]—dc22   2008011224
ISBN 978-1-4424-1244-6 (proprietary pbk)

El primer invierno de Chaucer

Chaucer's First Winter

STEPHEN KRENSKY · ILLUSTRATED BY HENRY COLE
ILUSTRADO POR

Simon & Schuster Books for Young Readers

New York   London   Toronto   Sydney

Chaucer was a curious young bear.
He poked and prodded wherever he pleased—
    under rocks, under water, even high in the trees.

Chaucer era un osito curioso.
Fisgoneaba y aguijoneaba donde se le antojaba—
    debajo de las rocas, bajo el agua, hasta bien alto
    en los árboles.

Chaucer's best friends were Nugget and Kit.
They were a little older than he was.

Los mejores amigos de Chaucer eran Nugget y Kit.
Eran un poquito mayores que él.

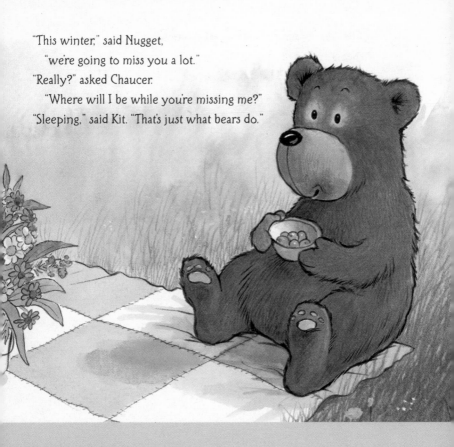

"This winter," said Nugget,
   "we're going to miss you a lot."
"Really?" asked Chaucer.
   "Where will I be while you're missing me?"
"Sleeping," said Kit. "That's just what bears do."

—Este invierno—, dijo Nugget.
   —te vamos a echar mucho de menos.
—¿De veras?—preguntó Chaucer.
   —¿Dónde voy a estar cuando ustedes me
van a echar de menos?
—Durmiendo—, dijo Kit—. Eso es justamente
lo que hacen los osos.

Chaucer's parents admitted that this news was true.
"Bears do like to snooze," his father observed.
"It's very restful," his mother added,
   "which is good for growing bears."

Chaucer was not convinced.

Los padres de Chaucer reconocieron que este dato era cierto.
—A los osos les gusta dormitar—, observó su papá.
—Es muy descansado—, añadió su mama—,
   lo cual es bueno para los ositos que están creciendo.

Esto no convenció a Chaucer.

Pretty soon, it was time for the bears' winter nap.
Chaucer's parents closed their eyes and began
    softly snoring.
Chaucer was still wide awake.

Poco después, fue hora de la dormitación de invierno
    de los osos.
Los padres de Chaucer cerraron los ojos y empezaro
    a roncar suavemente.
Chaucer seguía completamente despierto.

So he stood up. He stretched.
Then he went back outside.

Así que se levantó. Se estrechó.
Luego volvió a salir.

White flakes were tumbling through the air.
Chaucer caught one on his nose and two on his tongue.
They were wet to the touch and then melted away.
"It's magic," he said.

Por el aire daban vueltas unos copitos blancos.
Chaucer agarró uno en la nariz y dos en la lengua.
Eran fríos al tacto y luego se deslieron.
"Es pura magia", se dijo.

His friends were very surprised to see him.
"Why aren't you sleeping?" asked Nugget.

Sus amigos se asombraron al verlo.
—¿Por qué no estás durmiendo?— le preguntó Nugget.

"I was curious," said Chaucer. "I wanted to see what winter was all about."
Kit nodded. "Well, first we must teach you what to know about snow."

Chaucer was ready.

—Me dio curiosidad —, dijo Chaucer—.
    Quería ver qué es eso del invierno.
    Kit asintió con la cabeza. —Pues, primero
    tenemos que enseñarte lo que hay que saber
    sobre la nieve.

Chaucer estaba listo.

Chaucer saw that snow made everything look different.

"It's like the land is wearing a disguise," he thought.

He paused uncertainly at the top of one familiar hill.

"How do we get to the bottom?" he asked.

"You'll see," said Kit.

Chaucer notó que la nieve hacía que todo se viera distinto.

"Es como si la tierra se disfrazara", pensó.

Vaciló inseguro en la cima de una colina conocida.

—¿Cómo llegamos abajo?— preguntó.

—Ya versa—, le dijo Kit.

And they had themselves a wild ride.

Y tuvieron una bajada memorable.

Over the next few days Chaucer
    learned all about snowball fights.

*Durante los días siguientes Chaucer aprendió todo lo que hay que
    saber sobre las peleas con bolas de nieve.*

After a month, the pond froze over.
"Careful," said Nugget, as they stepped out.
Kit nodded. "You have to get used to it."

Un mes después, la laguna se congeló.
—Cuidado—, dijo Nugget cuando iban a caminar.
Kit asintió con la cabeza. —Tienes que acostumbrarte.

Chaucer's paws felt funny on the ice.

He was much better at sliding than gliding.

Las patas de Chaucer se sentían raras en el hielo.

Le era más fácil deslizarse que planear.

Chaucer loved everything about winter—
the glittering rows of icicles, the pine trees dressed in white.

A Chaucer le encantó todo lo del invierno—
las relucientes hileras de carámbanos, los pinos vestidos de blanco.

He even enjoyed the coldest winter nights.

Hasta disfrutó las noches más frías del invierno.

One gray morning, Chaucer, Nugget,
    and Kit were out exploring.
It started to snow. And it started to blow.
Chaucer sniffed the air deeply and began
    making giant snowballs.
"This is not a good time to play," said Kit.

Una mañana gris, Chaucer, Nugget
    y Kit se fueron a explorar.
Empezó a nevar. Y empezó a soplar.
Chaucer husmeó el aire profundamente
    y empezó a hacer unas gigantescas bolas de nieve.
—Éste no es buen momento para jugar—, dijo Kit.

But Chaucer knew what he was doing.

Pero Chaucer sabía lo que hacía.

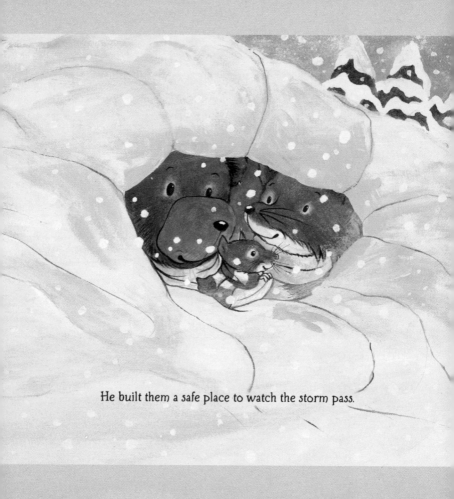

He built them a safe place to watch the storm pass.

Construyó un refugio para ver pasar la tormenta.

The storms grew gentler after that.
The sun got stronger and the days
   seemed longer.
"There's a change coming," said Nugget.
Kit took a deep breath. "I can almost
   smell the flowers."

But Chaucer was sorry to see winter go.

La tormenta se apaciguó después de eso.
El sol se fortaleció y los días parecían
   más largos.
—Viene un cambio—, dijo Nugget.
Kit respiró profundamente. —Casi puedo
   oler las flores.

Pero a Chaucer le afligía ver que el invierno se iba.

Chaucer headed back to his family's cave.
When he got there, his parents seemed to be
   just waking up.

Chaucer se encaminó a la cueva de su familia.
Cuando llegó, parecía como que sus padres
   apenas se despertaban.

"Wait till you hear about winter!"
    said Chaucer. "There's so much to do."
"Really?" asked his mother.
"Who would have guessed?" his father added.
Chaucer wanted to tell them all about snow
    and ice and sledding down hills.
He really did.

—¡Esperen que les cuente sobre el invierno!—dijo Chaucer—. Hay tanto que hacer.
—¿De veras?— preguntó su mamá.
—¿Quién lo hubiera adivinado?— añadió su papá.
Chaucer quería contarles todo sobre la nieve y el hielo y deslizarse cuesta abajo.
De veras que sí.

But the rest of his story was going to have to wait.

Pero el resto del cuento iba a tener que esperar.